Sentient Pen15 From Outer Space

Sabrina Cross

 Formatted with Vellum

*To everyone who has been told that's a terrible
idea:
I hope you do it anyway.*

Author's Note

This is a sentient object romance. Humans will be getting it on with sentient objects. Don't worry, everyone is gleefully consenting.

If you read the last three sentences and think that's not for you, that's okay. There is still time to put this book down and walk away. No one will blame you. It's the sane thing to do.

But if you're going to stick around please be aware of the following: No peens were harmed in the making of this book but there is some light self-harm directed at the sentient peen. Consent is important to these characters but there is some dubious consent moments with regards to the sentient peen and aphrodisiac usage. Talk of insanity and suicide caused by parasites.

If you feel I am missing anything please reach out to me at authorsabrinacross@gmail.com and let me know. A complete list can be found at www.sabrinacross.com

Chapter 1

Bane

"**A**re you kidding me? You can't go around poking people! We've talked about this, Bane." Liam's voice was low and aggravated as he hustled through the house and out the front door. The man was so high-strung. It'd be less annoying if I wasn't stuck with the guy.

Chill out, man, it wasn't that big of a deal. She wasn't complaining, was she?

"That doesn't matter! I care!"

Blah blah blah blah.

It was always the same with this guy. He wasn't interested in meeting women. He wasn't interested in meeting anyone. A hole was a hole to me. I didn't much care about the package, but Liam had *standards*.

Disgusting.

You're going to have to do it at some point. You know you can only hold out for so long.

It wasn't true. Liam had the constitution of a

priest. And it was all his fault. There was always a willing body.

"I know you don't care about all of the consequences of fucking your way through the city, but one of us has to."

Consequences are for losers.

"Easy for you to say, Bane. Fucking asshole."

"Oh, hey Liam. Are you leaving already?"

I couldn't help but perk up at the voice, even though she wasn't talking to me. Sibyl never talked to me. It didn't matter. Liam liked her and if there was ever a chance for us to break out of this chastity cycle, it was Sibyl.

"Uh, yeah. I'm not feeling great." Liam's voice was pitchy and weird. I didn't get it. Sibyl was cute enough, I supposed, in a wholesome, girl next door way. It made no sense Liam lost his nerve over this girl.

"I'm so sorry to hear that," she glanced over toward the house we had just vacated and gestured toward it with her thumb. It was an awkward move that made me want to roll my eyes. "I guess I should get in there. Feel better, Liam."

"Have fun, Sibyl." Liam said awkwardly, sliding his hands into his pockets. "See you around."

We waited until Sibyl was up the walk and at the door before turning away and starting back to the car.

"Why do you always do that shit?" He demands, his voice a harsh whisper meant only for me.

Do what?

I was playing dumb. I knew what he meant. I just wanted to hear him say it.

"You make it so fucking awkward. Can't you be chill around her for five fucking minutes?"

I'm not the one who can't be chill.

In fact, there was little about the woman that did it for me. It was entirely Liam's *emotions* that caused me to react whenever she was around. He was either too stubborn or too dense to realize he had the massive hots for the girl next door.

"I swear to all you hold dear, if you don't stop embarrassing me, I'm going to become a eunuch."

I slumped, deflated at the very idea. I could have argued. I could have tried again to make him realize he was the one making it awkward around Sibyl. But there was no talking to him when he was in that mood. And while I was fairly confident he wouldn't actually cut me off, I wasn't willing to risk it.

Chapter 2

Liam

S *he looks nice.* Bane whispered. I ignored him and the athletic blond he indicated. *What about her?*

Just as I ignored him when he pointed out every semi-attractive woman we passed in the grocery store. He kept urging me to chat them up, but it wasn't going to happen. No woman wanted to be hit on in the grocery store.

"Can't you keep it in your pants for five fucking minutes?" I snarled at him once safely secured in the car.

You keep it in your pants enough for the both of us. Bane shot back.

I rolled my eyes and started the car. "I'm sorry anonymous sex doesn't do it for me."

It doesn't have to be anonymous. Just give Sibyl a call.

"Fuck you," I told him before I put the car in drive and headed home.

It wasn't like I didn't want Sibyl. We'd lived

next door to each other nearly our whole lives until six years ago, when she'd decided she needed to do something more with her life and went to teach English as a second language in South America.

I still lived next door to her parents. Bought my childhood home from my own parents when they'd decided it was time to retire to Arizona a few years back. I could have kept my old apartment in the city, but I liked being back in the old house. It held a lot of great memories, and there was something about being there I'd never found living on my own.

It was comfortable, and allowed me to work in peace. I didn't have neighbors asking me about my roommate because they could hear me talking to Bane through the paper-thin walls. And I liked it more than ever, now that Sibyl was back next door.

She came home from her last teaching assignment and decided it was time to stay. Sibyl said it was because she wanted to settle down, but I knew it had more to do with her parents getting older and worrying about them being alone. She told everyone she was living at home to save money for a down payment on a house. The Sibyl I'd known would have savings and while everyone knew teachers didn't make shit, I didn't doubt for a minute she'd be able to afford a small apartment if she'd wanted to.

Whatever her reasons, it was nice having her back next door. Even though it was torture at the same time. Unrequited crushes went like that.

Sibyl had dated the same guy through most of middle school and high school. They broke up at the end of senior year when her boyfriend got a scholarship to an out-of-state university and decided he didn't want a girlfriend holding him back. Last I'd checked, Chet was divorced and his wife had taken him to the cleaners because he still couldn't keep it in his pants.

There had been a moment the summer before university I thought maybe something would happen, but I'd chickened out. The same way I'd chickened out before asking her to the seventh grade dance and she'd gone with Chet.

I'm sorry. I won't talk about Sibyl.

ignored Bane as I pulled into the driveway and cursed. Of course, the woman in question would be standing in the front yard wearing a sundress and getting damp in the gentle spray of the hose blowing back on her in the wind.

She looked so fucking good with her skirt blowing in the breeze and giving me teasing glances at her thighs. Thighs I wanted to mold with my hands, bite, feel crushing my face as I ate her pussy like it was my last meal.

Fuck. Fuck, fuck, fuck. I was no better than Bane.

You can't ignore your need forever. It isn't healthy. Not for either of us.

Actually, I could. I wasn't celibate to spite him, despite what Bane thought. It was just that I didn't know how to explain Bane or our relationship and it never felt right lying to women.

If you don't fuck someone soon, it's going to become a problem.

"It hasn't been a problem so far. Just control your fucking self, will you? Don't make it weird." With the final warning, I turned off the car and got out.

Chapter 3

Sibyl

My hand clenched on the hose trigger and I nearly drowned my mother's prized hydrangeas as I fought down the nerves buzzing in my belly. After missing Liam at the party the other night, I'd popped in long enough to say hi and have a single drink before going home to yell at myself for being such a loser. Again.

This was the first time I'd seen him since the party. So maybe his somewhat flimsy excuse of not feeling well was true, and he had been sick. But I'd learned from my casual stalking Liam didn't exactly keep regular hours.

Well, my friends called it stalking. I called it being a good neighbor and concerned for my childhood friend. It was with said friends' voices in my ears telling me to stop being a weirdo and get it, that I dropped the hose and headed toward the car where Liam was getting his groceries from the trunk.

It was time to woman up and do something

about this annoying crush. I was a nearly thirty-year-old woman. There was no reason to be moon-eyed over some guy. I'd feel him out and maybe, if I was lucky and he was into it, I'd get to feel him up.

"Hey there neighbor, feeling better?" I leaned against the side of the sleek black car and pressed my hands against the side. It was a move that shoved my chest out and made my tits look amazing in the pink sundress I'd picked.

"Hi Sibyl," Liam froze with his hands loaded up with bags. There were a couple left in the trunk, so I moved around to grab them. It would give me an excuse to follow him inside. "Yeah, much better. Thanks. Oh, you don't have to do that."

"I want to." I hefted the reusable bags into my arms and closed the trunk. "Lead the way."

"Uh, yeah, okay." He gave me a small smile before leading the way up the path to the front door. This was it, I was getting inside of Liam's house and then I was going to do my damndest to get inside of his pants.

"It's a bit of a mess, sorry." Liam dropped part of his load to unlock the front door and push it open for me.

I couldn't help but look around the space as we passed through to the kitchen. A few things were quickly apparent. First, he hadn't changed practically anything since he bought the house a couple of years ago. I hadn't been in the house in nearly a decade, but other than a new couch and

TV and the lack of family photos on the wall, it looked almost exactly as it had when his parents lived there.

Second, we had very different definitions of messy. There were a pair of sneakers by the front door, a hoodie tossed over the back of a recliner, and a glass on the coffee table, but nothing else in the living room was out of place. No books piled on the table, no blanket left balled up on the couch or chair.

The kitchen was much the same. There were a few dishes in the sink and the coffeepot was still half-full, but otherwise it was surprisingly neat. Annoyingly neat.

"Thanks for helping," Liam said, depositing his bags on the center island. I followed his lead and did the same with mine before I started looking through them for cold items. I could claim it was habit but I was being nosy.

I was so curious about the man my nerdy neighbor had become. We'd been close friends as children and I'd loved our days playing in our yards or video games in his living room. I'd been home for a few months and still hadn't managed to catch up with him at all.

The sane part of my brain said he was ignoring me for a reason and I should stop trying. But there was the nostalgic part of me that still wondered what might have happened if I'd asked him to the seventh grade dance instead of simply agreeing to go with Chet.

"Anytime, neighbor." I set the milk and eggs

on the island for Liam to put in the fridge. "Are you working this afternoon?"

"I'm kind of between projects right now." From anyone else our age, it would have been a giant red flag. But not Liam.

Never one to do the normal thing, he'd dropped out of college after a year and had started a cold case murder podcast. Much to almost everyone's surprise, it had taken off. Everyone except for me.

Liam had always been curious. He'd spent so much time researching local mines, mysteries, and murders as a kid. It hadn't surprised me at all he'd made a career out of it. Add in the fact he had a low, gravely voice, his podcast had been destined for success. Women everywhere had listened for his voice alone.

He'd gone from podcaster to nearly overnight success when he'd solved a cold case. And then another. In the last seven years, he'd written two books on popular cold cases he'd somehow figured out when the police couldn't. He'd done another one on a popular serial killer who hadn't allowed anyone to interview them before Liam. My mom told me he'd been offered jobs at both the FBI and CIA, but he turned them down.

He wasn't a millionaire or anything. I didn't think. But, he was more well off than most people in the small town we'd grown up in. I was still dying to know what brought him back here when he probably could have lived anywhere he wanted.

"Oh," was all I said. Smooth Syb.

We put the groceries away in silence. It was easy for me to help since he hadn't changed anything in the kitchen either. Everything was still stored exactly where his mother had kept it when we were kids.

"Did you change anything in here at all?" I asked. There was still an old phone book in the drawer, below where the phone used to be attached to the wall.

"The master bedroom is now my office," Liam shrugged. "My parents didn't want to move everything and it's comfortable, I know where things are. It works."

Silence stretched awkwardly between us. Liam shifted on his feet and I knew he was about to see me out. That was it. That was my chance to make a move or move the fuck on.

"Thanks for your help." He shifted again, glancing toward the door. Now or never, Syb.

"Yeah, no problem." I bit my lip and took a step toward him. I'd played this out a million times in my head. A million scenarios. And now the moment had come. I didn't have the slightest idea what to do.

Chapter 4

Liam

Kiss *her.* Bane growled into my head. I ignored him, like I always did. It was so much harder to do when he was saying the exact thing I wanted to do.

"We should get dinner sometime. Catch up. It's been a while and it feels like we're always missing each other." Sibyl bit her lip again and I had to swallow back a groan. I wanted to sink my teeth into that plump lower lip. I wanted to lick the sting away. I wanted to fill my hands with the plump curves of her thighs and ass.

Fuck. Fuck. Fuck!

I needed to get her out of there. I was either going to embarrass myself or I was going to fall on her like a starving dog on a steak. I bet she tasted so damn sweet.

"Yeah, that sounds good." I gestured her toward the door. "I've got some work to do now but I'll text you later."

"I thought you said you were between

projects." There was a little line between her brows I wanted to kiss away. It'd been thirteen freaking years, and this girl was still the only one that made me come completely undone.

Not for the first time, I hated Bane and what he'd done to me. Hated him for missing out on normal life experiences. But mostly, I hated him for taking away even the slightest chance I'd ever had with Sibyl.

"There's always work. Even when I'm not writing or in-season there's marketing and net-working to be done. Planning for the next season. Research."

"Oh," was I imagining the disappointment? "Well, I guess I'll leave you to it."

She started toward the kitchen door. I fell into step with her, ready to lock her and tempta-tion out, as soon as I could. She pulled the door open, and I nearly walked into her when she slammed the door and whirled around.

"You know what, fuck it." She fisted her hand in my shirt and pulled me down to her height. Her mouth crashed onto mine and I froze. What the fuck?

Kiss her, you fucking moron! Bane yelled. And, for the first time ever, I listened.

I did what I'd been imagining for years and grabbed a handful of her sable hair and pressed my mouth to hers in a bruising kiss. My other hand went around her waist, slid to her ass to cup the curve.

She let out a small whine before releasing my

shirt and locking her arms around my neck. I released her hair to cup her other cheek and haul her up against me. I pressed her into my aching cock.

That's it! You give it to her good.

I ignored Bane and focused all of my attention on the woman in my arms. The woman who had been the star of all of my teenage, and more than a few of my adult, fantasies.

The little wiggle she kept doing to grind against my cock was almost too much to bear. I may be a sexual monk, but I wasn't a teenager about to come in my pants. I hauled her up by my grip on her ass and carried her back to the island and set her down. After breaking our kiss, my lips moved down her neck and across her exposed collarbone.

"Oh, my god. Yes!" Sibyl's hands fisted in my hair and I let her guide my mouth across the slope of her breast to the peak. I tugged the triangle of her dress aside, pleased to find her bare beneath it. The rose of her nipple against her pale skin had my mouth watering for a taste.

Thankfully, she didn't make me beg. Sibyl used her grasp in my hair to drag my mouth to her peak. I'd never imagined I'd like being dominated by my partner, but fuck if her taking charge didn't make my cock twitch.

Gotta love a girl who demands what she wants. We're going to fuck her, right?

I continued to ignore Bane as I dragged my tongue over her nipple. I circled the areola before taking the hard peak into my mouth to suck.

"Oh, yes." Sibyl's hand fisted in my hair as she arched her back, offering herself up to me. I was impossibly hard and Bane was begging to get inside of her. For once, I agreed with him.

I tugged down the straps of her dress until I could lift both breasts out of the fabric. As I sucked the one, I pinched and rolled the other in my fingers. I increased pressure, pinching hard. Sibyl's grip tightened in my hair as she let out a loud moan.

Fuuuuuck. She likes it rough. Bane groaned into my head. *Who thought the girl next door would like it a little dirty?*

I wanted to yell at him to shut up, but our mental communication only went one way and there was no way to explain why I was telling an invisible force to shut the fuck up. Not when my mouth was busy licking across Sibyl's exposed flesh. Not when I could be using it to bring her pleasure.

"Off." Sibyl pushed up the hem of my shirt, shoving it over my stomach. "I want it off."

Happy to oblige, I tugged the shirt over my head and dropped it to the floor. Her hands were on me instantly. They dragged down over my pecs and down my belly. I wasn't ripped. I stayed in well enough shape, but I didn't care enough to work for washboard abs. Based on the way her hands pressed to my sides and she bit her lip, Sibyl didn't seem to mind.

Chapter 5

Sibyl

Liam was better than I had imagined. I wanted to run my tongue from the slight indent of his belly button, down the trail of hair, and into the waistband of his low-slung shorts. I wanted to taste him so badly my mouth watered for it.

I knew for some women, giving head was transactional. It was something they did to please their man, or in exchange for their man going down on them. For me, giving head was a power trip.

There was nothing hotter than turning a man on. It was a heady thing to have someone trust enough to put their prized flesh into my mouth and trusting I wouldn't hurt them. I loved making them lose control. I pushed him back a step and slid down from the counter, brushing my body against his as I regained my feet.

Liam's hands grabbed my waist, holding me against him. My boobs pressed against his chest, the warm skin against my sensitive nipples had pleasure pooling low in my belly. Fuck, I wanted this man more than I'd ever wanted one before.

I slid my arms out of the straps dangling around my elbows before gripping the waistband of Liam's shorts.

"I want to taste you," I said, pressing a kiss to his chest.

"Oh, fuck Sibyl." He gripped my wrists, stopping me from shoving his pants down. "I want to taste you first."

"Ladies first," I shot back, sliding to my knees. I looked up at him, my hands still gripped on his waistband, and waited. He groaned and the grip on my wrists went slack. I dragged his shorts down over his hips, slowly, taking my time to reveal him.

And oh, fuck. It was worth the wait. I slid his shorts down to his ankles and slid my hands up his thighs to frame his groin. My mouth watered as I wrapped my hand around the base of his dick and brought it to my lips.

"Did...did your penis just growl at me?" I sat back on my heels as my hands fell away from Liam's hard cock. It jutted out from a bed of trim curls. He was gloriously hard, curving up, pre-cum already beaded at the tip.

It was probably the prettiest penis I had ever seen and, until two seconds ago, I was fully prepared and eager to put it in my mouth. Except, I was fairly fucking certain it had growled at me.

"What? No, that's insane." Liam gripped his

cock and gave it one slow pump that had my gaze riveted. "It was definitely my stomach."

Which I might have believed. Except Liam could not lie worth a damn and he was absolutely lying to me. I might have been willing to write it off as horny weirdness from someone who had already told me it had been years since the last time he'd been with a woman. Except, I was pretty sure he had a growling penis, and we really needed to explore that.

"Liam?" I looked up the length of his body to his eyes. They were dark and half-shut as his hand gave another slow pump. "Want to tell me about your growling penis?"

His head fell backward on a curse and he looked up at the ceiling as though it might hold the answers I was demanding. Eventually, he blew out a breath and looked back down at me.

"No, talking about Bane is the very last fucking thing I want to do when your mouth is inches from my bare cock. When you've had your hands wrapped around him already and he's begging for more of it."

"Your penis has a name?" It wasn't the weirdest thing I'd ever heard of. One of my exes called his cock the matador, of all fucking things.

"A fucking nuisance, is what he is." Liam muttered before releasing his cock and propping his hands on his hips. "Might as well say hello."

My brow furrowed. He wanted me to talk to his cock? The cock he named Bane? I wondered if anyone else knew Liam Hurst was absolutely fucking bonkers.

I pressed my hands to the floor, ready to push to my feet and get the fuck out of there and away from the crazy person.

"Hello Sibyl, nice to officially meet you." The drop of pre-cum dropped to the floor as the hole of Liam's cock opened and closed with the words. Every joke or thought I'd ever had about the cock hole looking like a little mouth ran through my head.

It was the last thought I had before everything went black.

Chapter 6

Liam

I dove forward to catch Sibyl as she fell forward, barely managing to avoid hitting her in the face with my still-hard cock. I eased her to the ground and straightened her legs so she wouldn't wake up with numb feet.

"Look what you've done," I snarled at my stupid fucking penis as I yanked my shorts up.

"You told me to say hi." Bane's voice was harsh, defensive, and slightly muffled. "I said hi. It's not my fault she passed out."

"I didn't mean it! Are you insane? Of course she was going to pass out when a fucking cock started talking to her. Why would you do that? You never talk to them."

I grabbed a blanket off the couch and wrapped it around her. I thought about moving her to the couch, but I didn't want to risk hurting her.

"You've never invited me to before." I could hear the shrug in his voice and not for the first time, I debated the pros and cons of punching him. Except, that would only cause me pain, and I wasn't a masochist.

"What the fuck were you hoping to achieve? Did you want to send her running?" I tugged my shirt back on, not wanting to be naked when she woke up. I thought about fixing her top, but decided it would be better if I didn't try to wrangle her breasts into the small cups when she was unconscious.

"I was hoping to fuck her. I knew you wouldn't let it go that far if she didn't know about me, you never do, so I took my shot."

I glared down at him. "And how did that work out for you?"

"She's still here, isn't she?"

"She's fucking unconscious!"

"But she didn't run away." I could hear the shrug in his voice again. "It's a start."

Sibyl groaned and raised a hand to her head. I crossed the kitchen to sit down at her side, just as her eyes opened.

"Liam? What?" She jerked up, her gaze going straight to my covered cock. "Your penis talked. Which is insane, so clearly I'm going insane."

I tried to take her hand, but she jerked away from me. It hurt, but I couldn't say I blamed her.

"You're not going insane. It's—it's complicated."

"I had a hallucination that your penis was talking to me. I'm pretty sure that means I'm going insane. Or maybe there's a gas leak in your house. That can cause hallucinations, right? Maybe we should call the fire department."

She looked around the room. As if a phone, or possibly the fire department, would simply materialize out of nowhere. Meanwhile, I took stock of her.

Sibyl was pale. Her eyes were a little wild, a little glassy. Otherwise, she looked okay. Not like someone about to faint again.

"There's no gas leak. Can we maybe sit down and talk? I can explain."

"You can explain how your penis talked to me? There's some sort of reasonable explanation for that?"

"Reasonable? No." I got to my feet and offered her my hands. She stared at them for a long time before accepting one of them to pull her up. Her other hand kept the blanket clutched to her chest.

"Absolutely nothing about Bane is reasonable, so I cannot give you a reasonable explanation but I can give you the truth." I just hoped it would be enough.

Chapter 7

Bane

Liam was going to ruin this for us. Again.

I hung in defeated disdain between Liam's thighs as he walked Sibyl through the house to the living room. He kept his attention off of her ass as it swayed in front of us under that short little skirt.

There was no way the dude was going to explain our situation in a way that didn't have Sibyl running from the house and never coming back. We'd be lucky if she didn't either call the funny farm or the government scientist people who would certainly take us into custody to study or dissect us. We would not be going out like that.

Let me talk to her. I demanded. I kept it to Liam's mind, not wanting to scare Sibyl more than she already was.

"Not happening." Liam muttered. Sibyl looked over her shoulder at us, 'What the fuck' stamped across her pretty features. But she didn't bolt for the door, so it was a start.

"So, your penis is named Bane?" Sibyl sat on the couch and wrapped the blanket around herself. From the way she moved underneath it, I could tell she was putting her dress back on. Shame.

"Oh, don't give me that look. I didn't name him."

Sibyl's eyebrows rose in a clear call of bullshit. The girl had more sass and spine than I gave her credit. She may look like the sweet girl next door, but there was some heat under her sweet exterior. I wanted to unwrap her and discover it. I wanted to bury myself in it.

"Trust me, I wouldn't have named my penis Bane. I wouldn't have named my penis at all if it hadn't started talking to me." Liam dropped down on the coffee table across from the couch and propped his elbows on his knees with his hands dangling between them.

"Mmm-hmm, and that started about when?" Sibyl sounded like she was talking to a small child. Or a crazy person.

It was clear she was already trying to rationalize away what she'd seen. Clearly, she hadn't heard a penis growl at her. It must have been Liam's stomach. Obviously, it hadn't talked to her. She was lightheaded with pleasure, dizzy, imagining things.

She's deluding herself. Don't let her get away with it. I told Liam, begging him to do this right. To convince her I was real and here.

Once again, I cursed myself and the universe

for landing me in my current situation. It was unnatural. I was the superior being in Liam's body, but he'd maintained nearly all of his control.

When the others had taken hosts, they'd had partial control of the human. Sure, they'd driven the human host mad within months while Liam and I had been together for years, but that was a compatibility issue. I was sure of it.

"I've had Bane since I was thirteen." Liam ignored me, again, and spoke directly to Sibyl. I was getting really fucking tired of being ignored.

Chapter 8

Sibyl

I tried to think about Liam at thirteen. While we'd been close as kids, we'd grown apart in our teen years. I'd gotten wrapped up in dating Chet and being the perfect football player's girl-friend and Liam had...

Liam had apparently gotten a talking penis, and I hadn't had the slightest clue. To be fair, it wasn't like I'd had any contact with Liam's penis back then. No matter how much I'd thought about it, he'd never given any indication he'd been interested.

"Do you remember the old stories about the mines? Why they closed 'em up?" Liam twisted a silver band he wore on his index finger around as he talked.

"Of course, they started making people go crazy." The town had been a booming mining town for generations until the late forties, when suddenly workers started going insane. They'd assumed there was gas in the tunnels or something, and eventually the mining company shut down and closed off all access points. Dozens of miners had died before that, though.

"I'm going to need you to bear with me when I say this because I do realize how bat shit fucking crazy I sound, but it wasn't gasses making the miners go insane. It was the aliens."

The sound that escaped me was not ladylike or sexy, and under any other circumstances, I might have been embarrassed by it. But seriously, Liam was sitting there looking all sexy and solemn and serious, talking about aliens driving miners mad. It was bonkers. It was insane. It was impossible.

I started laughing and couldn't stop. The man of my dreams, the boy I'd had a crush on since the moment I realized boys weren't gross, was a fucking lunatic.

"Look Sib, I know it's insane. Do you think I haven't tried to come up with a reasonable answer over the years?" He dropped his head into his hands and drove his fingers through his hair. Liam looked up at me from beneath his lashes and the laughter died in my chest.

"I think you're fucking with me." I shoved my hair out of my face. This was an absolutely ridiculous conversation. "Aliens were not possessing miners and driving them insane. That's insane. Everyone knows it was the gasses in the tunnels."

"Right, the gasses that were released from the open-air cavern they found just before the problems began? The open-air cavern in the middle of nowhere that's completely inaccessible from the outside world? The cavern that had been mysteriously empty of wildlife and flora? That cavern?"

That was it. I'd had enough. Whatever it was I had thought I'd seen or heard in the kitchen was probably the excitement of the moment. Penises didn't talk. Or growl. Boys did not get possessed by aliens. Liam was fucking with me and I was not going to sit there and let him get away with it.

"Look, if you didn't want to fuck me, you could have just said so. You didn't have to mock me." I shoved to my feet and threw the blanket at him. "I don't know when you became such a fucking asshole, Liam, but you're not the guy I thought you were."

"Don't be a fucking drama queen. Sit down and listen." The voice was lower than Liam's, not just in register but from his body. Liam's mouth hadn't moved. "This loser wants to fuck you so bad he's stupid with it. It's his fucking morals getting in the way."

My legs gave out, and I dropped back onto the couch. Liam dropped the blanket and grabbed his cock through his shorts.

"Bane! You will not talk to her like that." His grip looked painful. His knuckles were white with the strength of his grasp. "Shut the fuck up."

"But, but, but... That's impossible!" I stared at his cock through his shorts. It was impossible. Impossible.

"There are more things in heaven and Earth

and all that." Liam said. He released his penis and dropped back down across from me. "Can you handle the rest or are you going to call me an asshole again?"

Chapter 9

Liam

I wasn't sure how I'd expected the conversation with Sibyl to go, but being called an asshole and having a blanket thrown in my face hadn't been on my list of outcomes. I also hadn't expected Bane to join the conversation. In the fifteen years since he'd invaded my body, he'd never once spoken to anyone else.

"I–I don't know. I don't understand." Sibyl's hands were shaking as she twined them together and untangled them over and over. I reached out to take them, but she jerked away. A pang shot through my heart, but I guessed I couldn't blame her. Not really.

"I get it, I do. I've had years to get used to it. But I want you to understand." Was it even possible for her to understand? Would she still want anything to do with me if she did?

Probably not. It was too much to expect her to understand, let alone want to take on.

"Stop pussyfooting around and tell her."

Bane said. I reached down and grabbed him again. It wasn't very effective, but it was the only thing I had. Sure, it hurt me, but it hurt him too and sometimes it was worth the pain.

"No, it, he, Bane is right." Sibyl grabbed my wrist and pulled my hand away. "Just tell me. This build up is worse, I think."

I wanted to grab her hand, but I let it drop when she released me. I twisted the ring on my finger as I thought about the best way to explain.

"Let me fucking do it," Bane snapped. He was more impatient than usual. And I couldn't quite get used to him speaking aloud. Even when we were alone, he usually preferred to speak into my mind.

"Oh," Sibyl looked at my cock, which stirred at her attention. It usually didn't take much to rile Bane up, but I knew my reaction to Sibyl didn't help matters. "I don't know..."

She looked up at me and bit at her lower lip. There was a question in her eyes I couldn't begin to understand. Whatever it was, I wanted to give it to her.

"Is he really only in your–" she gestured toward my crotch again, "Penis?"

"Kind of?" I wasn't sure how to explain our connection. Honestly, I didn't fully understand it myself. "He's part of me. The only part of my body he can control is my cock but he's everywhere."

I flexed my fingers, aware of the ghost sensation under my skin. Most of the time I could tune it out. But, if I focused, I could feel him. In the beginning, it had just been my dick, but over the years he'd invaded every cell of me. Our symbiotic relationship was so complete I was certain there was no separating us again.

"So when I touch you, he can feel it?" She traced her fingers up my forearm and goosebumps traced the wake of her touch.

"Yes," Bane replied before I could. His voice was raspier than usual. He'd enjoyed her touch as much as I had. It was new, but I could feel his pleasure in my chest.

"Interesting." She leaned back on the couch and eyed me up and down. "Weird. Okay, I think I'm ready for the rest."

She reached up and grabbed a lock of hair. The way she twirled it in her fingers was familiar. A gesture from our childhood I hadn't realized I missed. She might be saying she was ready, but she was nervous.

"I guess I'll go first," Bane said. I almost argued with him, but why not? It was as much his story as mine. He might as well start from the beginning. Maybe it would help Sibyl make sense of it.

"My planet was dying. Centuries ago now, the sun was going out and my galaxy was going dark. My kind escaped on a meteor. We're an adaptable species that require little resources to survive. We travelled for decades until the meteor we'd used to escape landed on this planet. We'd thought we'd finally be able to rebirth our kind, but we cannot survive here."

"Why not?" Sibyl asked my dick. She looked up at me. "I feel weird talking to him like this."

"Like what?"

"All covered up." She gestured at my shorts and my eyes popped wide at what she was saying.

"You want me to sit here with my cock out?"

"That's weird, right?" She nodded to herself. "Yeah, it's weird. But also, yes?"

I like her. Bane said into my mind at the same time he went fully erect under her attention. I didn't reply to him as I lifted my hips to slide my shorts down and off. The table was cool under my ass. It was almost worth it for the way Sibyl eyed my cock. There was discomfort and curiosity, but there was also hunger in those pretty, wide eyes.

"Thanks, it gets hot in there," Bane said, jumping a little. I clenched my hands around the edge of the table to keep from reacting. The blood rushing to my cock felt good, even if I wasn't in control of it. "Anyway, it's the sun. Your sun is too harsh for my kind. There were thousands of us when we'd left home and many of them died upon landing. They'd been so desperate when we'd landed they'd explored out without caution and burned under the brutal light."

Sibyl gasped, her hands coming to rest on her chest as she thought about the thousands of aliens she didn't believe in dying. That was the type of person she was.

"When we learned we could take hosts, there

had been hope. But the small animals that used to frequent the cave could only survive a matter of days before they expired. Their deaths took their host with them. Then the humans came."

"It was the miners," I explained, taking over from Bane. "I've seen the colony. It looks like black mold on the cave wall. The miners didn't go crazy. They were invaded. They were taken over by the parasitic mold and it drove them crazy."

"But not you?" The question was filled with skepticism. She clearly thought I had gone crazy. I didn't blame her.

"I have a talking penis that likes to whisper into my mind. I'm not totally unaffected." I pointed out. "But I am, at least, smart enough not to run around talking about my talking prick and making people think I'm nuts."

"I resent the prick comment," Bane said with an aggravated twitch. Sibyl and I ignored him.

"So you're telling me the people in this town didn't just go crazy one day after sucking down too many gases, but stumbled upon a parasitic space mold. That's the story you're going with?"

"He's right there. You've heard him talk. Have you been down in the mines sucking on gasses recently? What explanation can you come up with for why my cock is talking?"

"Aliens aren't real, Liam. I just can't believe that."

"You humans, all so self-centered. There's a big, wide universe out there, baby girl. You can bet more than one kind of lifeform exists."

I wanted to smack Bane for being rude, but he wasn't wrong.

"You're a talking penis!" Sibyl yelled back at him. She froze when she realized what she'd done. "Okay, point taken."

"I know it's crazy, I get it. But short of killing myself, I cannot be separated from Bane." I reached out and grabbed her hands. "I understand if it's too much for you. I do. It's a lot to take in. I won't blame you if you never speak to me again. But I need to make sure you don't tell anyone else."

"Who would believe me?" Sibyl said. She pulled her hands free from me and wiped them on her skirt. I would have been offended, but my hands were clammy. She was going to reject me.

Couldn't say I could blame her.

Chapter 10

Sibyl

I was insane. That was the only explanation for the fact I wasn't running screaming into the night. It was the only thing that explained why my gaze kept drifting down to Liam's cock. To Bane.

Oh god, his cock was infected by alien mold. And all I could do was sit there and think about riding him.

"Question. What about sex?" The words blurted out before I could think better of it or even how to phrase all of the questions in my head.

"I'm a big fan of it," Bane said.

"How would you know?" Liam shot back, glaring down at his dick.

"Why wouldn't he know?" My eyes went wide. "Are you saying-"

Oh, my god. Liam could not be a virgin. He couldn't. He was tall, broad, and gorgeous. He was a famous author and podcaster. There was no way he'd never had sex before.

"I couldn't." He shrugged, but the move was tight. "There was no way I could explain about Bane and it didn't feel right."

"But we—" I gestured back toward the kitchen.

"That got out of hand." He leaned forward, playing with his ring again. "I've never let it go that far. It was just, well, it was you, and you were kissing me, and... I'm sorry."

I goggled at him. I didn't have a high body count by any means, but I'd had my fair share of partners. I liked sex. A lot. I couldn't imagine never having it.

"Can you not at all?" I looked down at Bane. "Wouldn't it suffocate him?"

Liam and Bane both laughed. It was fucking weird looking at one person and hearing two distinct laughs.

"Oh, I definitely could."

"He's just a fucking monk with *morals*." Bane sneered morals out like it was a sin. A dirty word. It was clear Bane thought it was an insult, and I wasn't sure how I felt about it.

"Ignore him. Bane is a pleasure-seeking asshole." Liam wrapped his hand tightly around his cock. Again, the grasp looked painful. I couldn't stop my pussy from clenching at the sight, though.

"You would be too, you know," Bane growled out. "My kind doesn't feel sensation like yours does. I've lived for centuries and there was nothing remotely like pleasure during that time. You don't understand the pull of something so good when you've never had it before."

"Wanna bet?" Liam said under his breath. But his eyes were on me and they burned hot. Heat flashed over my body and pooled in my belly. I wanted him. Despite everything, I still wanted Liam.

"We could..." I trailed off. All of Liam's focus jumped to me, and I could feel it like a physical touch. I swallowed. "I mean, I would."

"I don't need a pity fuck, Sibyl." Liam's voice was harsh at the same time Bane gave an enthusiastic "yes!"

I pushed to my feet and crossed the step between us to straddle Liam's lap. I took his hands in mine and brought them to my thighs, just below where my skirt rested.

"Pity has nothing to do with what I'm feeling right now." I traced my fingers across the top of my dress, across the top of my breasts. "I came over here to fuck you, Liam. I want what I came for."

"I love a girl who knows what she wants," Bane said, his voice muffled by my weight. I could feel him jump against my covered pussy. Something about it made me giggle.

"It isn't just me," Liam reached down to grasp his penis. He dragged the head of it over my parted lower lips. "You're not just fucking me. You have to be okay with fucking Bane too."

Was I okay with that? I tried to think about the alien parasite living inside of Liam. It was his body on the outside, but he had another being inside of him. A very aware and opinionated being who would always be between us.

Liam continued to drag the head of his cock over me, making it hard to think about anything else. What would his cock feel like inside of me? How would Bane change that? He clearly had some control over Liam's cock. The way it jumped and twitched while we were talking wasn't typical.

I thought about Bane telling us his kind didn't feel pleasure and the fact Liam had never had sex before because he couldn't bring himself to bring someone else into it without them knowing. I'd spent so many nights imagining what it would be like to have sex with Liam and while this wasn't exactly how I'd envisioned it, I would be lying if I said I didn't still want it.

"I'm okay," I said. And I was. It was insane, but I was.

"If you change your mind, say stop. I'll stop."

I wasn't given a chance to respond before Liam's mouth crashed down on mine. His hand released his cock and moved to shove my panties aside. The way his thumb immediately found my clit told me he clearly hadn't been a total virgin over the years. No one who didn't have first-hand experience could have found and played that little bundle of nerves as well as he did.

It took moments before he had me squirming

and panting into his kiss. He didn't let up. A hand on the back of my head held me in place while he devoured me. His fingers curled around my underwear, anchoring my body as his thumb circled and pressed against my clit in perfect tempo. It was almost too much, but then his penis began tapping against the crease of my ass in hard thumps..

"Oh fuck," I wrenched my head away and back, groaning into the air as my body caught fire. Pleasure raced through me, igniting every nerve ending in its path. Liam's teeth closed around my neck and I was done for. The pleasure broke, washing over me in endless waves.

"I need you," I panted, grinding and shifting against Liam's grasp, trying to get the friction I needed. "Inside me. Now."

Instead of releasing my panties and slamming his cock into me like I'd expected, Liam shifted his grip until he could bury two fingers in my aching pussy. His groan matched my moan as I clenched around his invasion. His thumb kept a steady pressure on my clit as he began sliding his fingers deep and curling inside of me. His free hand moved to press against my ass under my skirt, holding me in place as my body began to shake.

"Fuck me," I moaned, grinding down against his hand. "Liam, fuck me."

"Can't." His words were a rasp against my skin. "Not yet."

He pressed deep and curled his fingers. They

pulsed against my g-spot and sent my eyes rolling back. My shaking legs gave out as the orgasm hit.

"Fuck," Liam said, fluttering his fingers inside of me. "That's right, come for me."

"Liam," I clung to his shoulders as I rode out the pleasure. "I want you."

"Soon, sweetheart." Liam continued to press and slide and circle his fingers and thumb, drawing out the pleasure as far as it would go.

I could feel his cock pressing against my ass and I wanted it inside of me so badly. I didn't understand why Liam was hesitating. I reached between us and moved to position him where I wanted him, but his hand circled my wrist.

"We don't have a condom." Liam said, eyes steady on mine.

"I have an IUD." I wriggled against him.

"Sibyl, I don't know enough about Bane's species to know if it's safe. We're not having sex without a condom." Fuck, I'd forgotten about that. I'd never considered the implications, but Liam was right. I didn't want to wake up tomorrow with my vagina talking to me because I'd been too horny to think.

"Let's get one, then. I want you to fuck me." I swirled my hips around the head of my cock, but let Liam pull my hand away from it. I could hear Bane's disappointed groan from beneath me.

"I know, sweetheart. But I don't have any." He brushed his fingers gently over my sensitive vulva. "There was no way I could have planned for this."

I dropped my head back and cursed up at the ceiling. I had never considered the idea Liam wouldn't have condoms. I didn't have any either. I was living at home and not dating, so I hadn't bought any since getting home earlier in the summer.

"My kind doesn't reproduce that way," Bane said, jumping up and pressing against my damp flesh.

Liam snorted. "Forgive me if I don't believe you."

I was with Liam. Bane seemed harmless enough, but he was still an alien species who had come to invade our planet. There was no way I was trusting anything he had to say on the subject.

Chapter 11

Liam

It was sheer torture to help Sibyl right her clothing and send her on her way. But with neither of us having condoms, it didn't seem like the best idea to stay together. We both came too close to throwing caution to the wind and my self-restraint was on a thin string.

I spent the afternoon cleaning the house, running to the store for some wine and flowers. And condoms. Lots and lots of condoms. The cashier smirked at me as they took the extra-large package from the security box. But I didn't care.

Assuming Sibyl didn't come to her senses and go running in the opposite direction, I was going to be having sex for the first time that night. Nothing was bringing me down. Not even a smirky kid who thought safe sex was something to laugh at.

By seven, my house was spotless. I had a salad in the fridge, steaks and baked potatoes warming in the oven. The bouquet of flowers I got from the grocery was on the table, along with a bottle of wine.

By seven-fifteen, I was about out of my mind. Sibyl was almost compulsively early. I couldn't remember a single time in our lives she was late.

"She's not coming." I told Bane, pouring myself a glass of wine. I glared at the flowers. I was an idiot.

Of course, she wasn't coming. Who in their right mind would want to get involved with us? Sure, I wasn't a bad looking guy and there was a certain fame involved with my job that drew women in. But who would want to stick around for the whole package of my life?

Women like to keep men guessing. Don't give up on her yet. Bane seemed so sure she was coming. I didn't share his faith. He didn't have the memories of Sibyl I had.

"Everything you know about women came from movies." I downed my glass of wine and poured another. I debated getting dinner out of the oven, but decided getting drunk would be easier on an empty stomach.

Your point?

"Your advice is shit." I took my wine to the living room and thought about putting on a movie, but was too restless for it. I could feel Bane under my skin, his energy making me fidgety.

Go after her. Bane demanded.

"If she wanted us, she'd be here." I thought about heading upstairs to work, but the idea didn't hold any appeal either.

I was still standing in the middle of the living room holding a glass of wine and debating what to do when my doorbell rang. I nearly flew across the room and down the hall to answer it. Still holding the now-empty wine glass, I opened the door. It fell to the floor when I laid my eyes on the girl next door.

Her brown hair hung down over one shoulder. Her wide mouth was painted a bright red. Her hazel eyes were dark and hot as they met mine. But what had me swallowing my tongue was her lace-encased body.

Under an open tan trench coat, red lace encased her curvy body. The lace dipped low between her tits. It hugged her softly rounded stomach, before nipping in to cover her pretty pussy. I wanted to be the lace between her thighs.

I grabbed her around the waist and hauled her inside and slammed the door shut. There was no way I wanted to risk anyone else seeing her like that. No, she was all for me.

"Sorry I'm late." She said, her voice a little breathless as I pushed her up against the door.

"I hadn't noticed." My hands slid over her curves and up to cup the barely covered tits. I wanted to bury my face in them. "Fuck, you're gorgeous."

If you don't fuck her this time, I'm going to make your life hell. Bane snarled.

I didn't bother to respond to him. Because there was no way we weren't going all the way this time.

"I'm late." She wrapped her arms around my neck and pressed that sweet little body against me. "I lost my nerve and changed too many times to admit."

"I'm so fucking happy you changed your mind. This was the best possible surprise." I couldn't stop touching her. Her skin was warm silk, the lace a soft contrast. My breath was caught in my chest as I slid my hands under the coat on her shoulders and shoved it to the ground. I'd forgotten all about the glass until the coat landed on it, but I'd take care of it later.

"So, dinner?" Sibyl asked. I pulled back to see amusement dancing in her eyes.

"Fuck food." I gripped her by her ass and hauled her up my body and into my arms. "No more waiting."

"Thank god."

I carried Sibyl through the house and up the stairs to my room. The light flooded in the windows and gave me a great view of her in the little lace tease. I tried to lay her down on the bed, but she stopped me.

"There's something I need to do." Sibyl said, demanding I put her on her feet. And then she dropped.

For the second time that day, Sibyl was on her knees in front of me. I was already speechless before she even wrapped her bright red lips around the head of my cock and sucked. My hands went to her head. It took everything in me not to force her movements. Not to hold her still and drive myself deep into her warm mouth.

Sybil's hand wrapped around the base of my cock, tightened and her nails dug into my ass as she moved her mouth over me.

Fuck! Bane growled into my mind, unable to speak with Sibyl's mouth surrounding him. I agreed. I never wanted this to end. *That's it, baby girl. Swallow me down.*

"Shut up," I told Bane, feeling weird, I was the only one who could hear him.

"Excuse me?" Sibyl glared up at me.

"Not you, sweetheart." I cupped her cheek and ran a thumb over her swollen bottom lip. Her lipstick smeared across her lip and my thumb. "You're perfect. Make all the noise you want."

"You are perfect," Bane told her. "You're doing so good, baby girl."

My cock twitched in Sibyl's hand, and her gaze dropped. Her tongue came out to lap at the drop of pre-cum on the head. My cock jumped again as Bane let out a moan to echo mine.

"There's something to be said for the surround sound praise," Sibyl said before she ran her tongue up from the base to tip. She closed her mouth over us again and it was almost too much to take when she released a moan.

It didn't take long for her teasing and sucking to have me at the edge. Bane's constant cursing in my head echoed my own feelings, and it somehow compounded into something more.

"I'm going to come," I grunted out from between clenched teeth. "Sweetheart, you have to stop."

Instead, her grip on my cock tightened to a nearly painful degree, and she sucked harder. My balls drew tight and the tingling at the base of my spine spread outward as my orgasm washed over me. My hands gripped Sibyl's head as I buried myself as deep as I could into her mouth. My cock throbbed as cum spurted out.

"Fuck!" I swore and jerked out of her mouth. Cum shot all over her face and tits. "I'm so sorry, Sibyl. I didn't mean to."

I dropped to my knees beside her.

Chapter 12

Sibyl

Warmth spread through my body. It started in my throat and moved down to pool in my belly. It spread across my skin. Desire raced behind it. Liam fell to his knees beside me and I barely noticed.

"Sweetheart, are you okay?" Liam touched my shoulder and I shuddered as heat flashed through me. "Sibyl?"

A whimper escaped me and I turned into his touch, needing more. Flames of desire licked over my skin and I was shaking with the need to be touched. I turned and crawled into Liam's lap.

"Please," I begged. I rubbed my body against him, but the touch was almost too much as my sensitive nipples brushed against his chest. Blood rushed to my pussy. It flooded my clit with warmth and made the little bud swell and beg for attention. My vagina clenched on nothing. I couldn't stop the whine as I ground myself awkwardly against Liam.

I didn't understand what was happening to me. It was too much and not enough at the same time. I needed release like I needed my next breath. I needed to be filled, fucked. I needed Liam to rail me until I couldn't feel my legs and then to do it again.

Liam's hands were on my hips. They held me in place while he stared at my face. Whatever he saw there, he didn't seem to like because he was frowning now. That look was not the look of a man about to fuck me every which way until Friday. It was unacceptable.

I reached down and grabbed his penis and aligned it between my lips so I could slide over the smooth flesh. It wasn't enough. I shifted to unsnap the crotch of my bodysuit before readjusting the position again. When his flesh rubbed against mine, I couldn't stop the moan.

"I need you, Liam. It aches." I rolled my hips, so he had no doubt about what was aching. "Make it feel better."

"What the fuck is happening to her?" He growled out. I didn't understand. I was there. He was pantless. I was pantless. Why was he not inside of me?

I pinched and tweaked at my nipples through the lace of my lingerie, still grinding down against Liam's cock. A cock that was still annoyingly not inside of me. I whined and shifted, trying to force him to fuck me.

Alarm bells were ringing in the back of my mind, but I couldn't understand them through the fever of desire that had me in a chokehold. Mmm, chokehold. I'd bet Liam's hands would feel great around my throat. Pinning me in place as he fucked me hard.

I rode harder, tilting my hips until my clit slid against his dick and into the neat, coarse hair against his pelvis with every movement. I abandoned my nipples to grip Liam's shoulders as I rode him. God, why wasn't he fucking me?

"Fuck you, Bane. Something is wrong with her. She's not even here." Liam's grip on my hips tried to slow my movements. I fought against him with a whine. I needed it. I needed him. I needed to make the heat go away. I needed something inside of me so badly I couldn't stand it. I could feel my wetness coat my thighs and Liam's cock. I was so ready for him.

Couldn't he see I was aching for his cock? I'd spent all afternoon and evening daydreaming about finally getting to fuck him and now we were alone and mostly naked and he wasn't fucking me. What was wrong with him?

"Why won't you fuck me?" My words were a pathetic whine, but I couldn't stop it. I felt pathetic. Pathetic and horny and desperate.

"It's okay, sweetheart. I'm going to take care of you." Liam shifted and lifted me off of him. I whined and tried to crawl back into his lap, but he kept me at bay as he got to his feet. With a surprising ease, he lifted me up and onto the bed. My hand went between my legs and I pushed two fingers inside of myself as I watched him unbutton his shirt and kick his leg free of his pants and boxers.

I was panting when he finally touched me. But he only pulled my lingerie off of me and tossed it aside with his clothes. Yes, great, perfect. We were both naked and his cock was standing at attention. It was at the perfect height for me to lean forward and lick it, so I did.

Liam cursed and yanked away. He wrapped his hand around his cock and pulled it tight against his body.

"I wanted that," I reached for him again but he grabbed both of my wrists and locked them together with one large hand.

"I know, sweetheart," He released his cock to cup my face. His eyes danced back and forth between mine, and I couldn't help but whine. Couldn't he see I was on fire? Didn't he know the only thing that would help me would be to stick his huge cock inside of me and fuck me until I couldn't move? "But you can't have any more of Bane tonight. Our cum doesn't seem to agree with you."

He leaned down and kissed the top of my head. I dropped my head back until I could meet his lips with mine. He gave me a soft kiss but didn't deepen it. I clenched my hands around his, needing to move them, needing to touch him. A low keening met my ears, and I realized it was coming from me.

"Please Liam, I need you." I pressed my legs together in an effort to get the friction I needed. It wasn't enough. My entire body was tense as a bowstring and I needed release.

"It'll be okay," Liam leaned me back, releasing my hands just long enough to change his grasp to lever them above my body. "I'm going to take care of you. I'm going to make it all better."

His touch was a brand, burning my body from the inside out. He slid his hand over me slowly, gently, before he cupped my mound. One finger spread me and pressed against my clit. My hips bucked at the gentle caress and I cried out.

"Shh, it'll be okay. I'm so sorry, sweetheart. We didn't know. We couldn't have guessed this would happen or we never would have let you near us." His fingers pressed and circled, shoving me straight to the edge and over.

I cried out when my pussy clamped on nothing. The emptiness was a hollow ache that left me unsatisfied. Liam seemed to understand my need, though. I had barely come down from my orgasm when he pushed two fingers inside of me. He fucked me hard and fast on his fingers.

He pushed me until my body was shaking and I was whining and panting non-stop before he added another finger. The stretch was intense and exactly what I needed. I gripped the sheets and writhed under his touch. When I came, he didn't stop. He kept thrusting and pressing, prolonging the orgasm until it rolled into another and another.

"Enough," I panted, my body limp and weak from multiple orgasms. My skin still burned, but I was too tired and weak for any more. "Please, I can't."

Liam pulled his fingers free of me. They were shiny with my juices. Strands of cum stretched from my body to his fingers and I grimaced. I'd never come so much in my life and I could feel it leaking out of me and pooling on the bed.

"I'll be right back," Liam pressed a kiss to my lips and climbed off the bed. I realized I was laying with my legs spread wide and dangling off the sides but I couldn't move. Every part of me was weak and exhausted.

I closed my eyes and swore I'd move in just a moment. Just as soon as I got feeling back in my limbs.

Chapter 13

Liam

Did you seriously just come in your pants? Bane's voice was disgusted.

"Technically, I wasn't wearing pants." I dampened a washcloth with warm water and cleaned the cum off of my stomach and cock before tossing it into the hamper and grabbed another to clean Sibyl up.

Pathetic.

I ignored Bane's sneer and headed back into the bedroom. I had made a woman I've been attracted to for years come so many times she passed out. Fuck yeah, I'd come too. Watching her writhe and shake beneath me was more than enough to get me off.

When I returned to the bedroom, Sibyl was exactly where I had left her. I shook her gently, but she didn't respond. Her heart rate was steady, and she was breathing okay. But she didn't react at all as I tried waking her.

"Should I be worried about this?" I gently

cleaned her up with the wet cloth and tossed it aside.

She appears to be sleeping. She will be fine.

I let out a long breath before I scooped the sleeping woman off my bed and settled her further up so she was no longer hanging off the edge. She didn't stir at all as I got her settled under the blankets.

"We can't let that happen again," I told Bane as I yanked on a pair of black boxer-briefs. "She was out of her mind."

You tried to warn her. Bane argued, as if it made everything okay. *I don't understand why you didn't fuck her. She was begging for it.*

"She wasn't begging for me. She was begging for release. Because you drugged her." I eyed Sibyl and decided she wasn't going to wake up anytime soon.

It wasn't like I knew this would happen. Bane was defensive.

It wasn't something I'd heard from him before. Maybe what had happened to Sibyl bothered him as much as it bothered me.

I headed downstairs to turn off the oven and transfer the food into the fridge for later. Once that was done and the dishes were stacked into the sink, I grabbed a couple bottles of water and a bottle of painkillers. I had no clue what state Sibyl would be in when she woke up and I wanted to be prepared.

Sibyl hadn't moved an inch when I returned to the bedroom. I thought about leaving her and going to crash on the couch, but I didn't want her to wake up alone. And, selfishly, I didn't want to miss a chance to sleep next to her. Especially because I was certain she wouldn't want anything to do with me come morning.

A soft, feminine moan woke me up. Well, that and the firm press of a plump ass against my cock. Sibyl wriggled closer and arched against me.

Oh, fuck. I had hoped after she passed out the lingering effects of the aphrodisiac in our cum would have cleared her system. I wasn't sure how much longer I could hold out with her begging me to fuck her.

So, just fuck her. Bane suggested. He stood at full attention and rubbed against Sibyl's rounded ass. Pleasure shot through me at the press of her bare flesh on my cock. A part of me wanted to listen to Bane. It wouldn't take much to lift her top leg and drape it over my hips. The position would leave her wide open and make it so easy to slide my cock deep inside of her.

But that would make me a monster. I wasn't going to take advantage of a woman I liked and respected. Especially not one who was clearly still drugged if the wriggling of her hips and little moans meant anything.

I reached out and put my hand on her bare hip. The blankets had been kicked away at some point and there was nothing hiding her soft curves. I gripped her rounded flesh and held tight, keeping her from moving against me.

"Sibyl, baby, you've got to stop."

Sibyl froze. Her head snapped toward me and her eyes went wide. She sat up and reached for the blanket tangled around our feet.

"Oh, my god. I am so sorry." She wrapped the blanket around her the best she could and every part of me was disappointed at the loss of all her soft, pale flesh. "I didn't mean to attack you in your sleep."

She started to get up,but I stopped her, grabbing her hand and pulled her back toward me. There was no way I was letting her out of the bed. Especially not thinking I was upset about her behavior. If she was back in her right mind, there was nothing I wanted more than to finish what we had started the day before.

I hauled her back into my arms, leaving the blanket wrapped around her. She made a har-rumphing sound but didn't fight me when I cra-dled her against my body.

"How are you feeling?" I ran a hand up and down her back, urging her even closer against me. "I'm so sorry about last night. We didn't know. I've never, I mean, well, it's never come up before."

"A little dehydrated but otherwise pretty good, actually. Kind of sore, but in a good way." She stretched and wiggled. I willed my body not to react, but Bane had other plans. He stood at attention, pressed against the curve of Sibyl's ass.

"Sorry," I said, shifting her a little, so she wasn't sitting directly on my cock.

"Don't be." Amusement twinkled in her eyes as she slid down and wriggled until she settled firmly over my cock again. "Yet again, we failed to finish what we started."

"So we did," I snaked a hand under the blanket and around to cup her breast. It overfilled my palm. "Are you sure you're up for this?"

"Oh my god, Liam! Will you just fuck me already?"

I couldn't hold back the laugh as she wrapped a hand around the back of my neck and pulled me down to her. She bit my lower lip before sliding her tongue over it and into my mouth.

"Only because you asked so nicely."

Chapter 14

Bane

Finally.

Fucking finally.

We were going to do it. We were going to have sex. Liam's heart was pounding and his hands shook as he helped Sibyl unwrap from the blanket and lay her out on the bed. She looked like a feast. She was soft and round. Her skin was soft under our touch.

Soft sensations were indescribable. For centuries, there had only been nothingness, pain, or fear. The excitement coursing through our body, the pleasure at Sibyl's touch, the anticipation of more. It was almost too much to bear.

There was something wrong with my connection with Liam. The others of my species who took a host had managed some level of control over them. At least in the beginning. As the humans' minds fought back, they'd lost control. Which was usually the point the human went insane and took their life or ended up heavily sedated.

Not a single one of them had spoken about the intense physical sensations associated with inhabiting a human. Had they not felt it? Had they wanted to keep that knowledge to themselves? Sometimes it was borderline overwhelming and made maintaining control difficult.

Whatever the reason, our connection was altered. It kept me from driving Liam insane. And it allowed me to feel what he was feeling. Some sensations were stronger than others. Direct contact with our cock was so intense it made my mind stutter. The further from that point, the less sensation I got. Touching Sibyl was pleasurable, but having her touching us was so much more.

I'd nearly lost control alongside Liam as she wrapped her lips around me. I wondered what it would be like, should I ever completely let go the way Liam had. For years, I'd had to maintain control to keep the connection with Liam. But we'd been together for so long by now, I wasn't sure anything could separate us.

Liam was sliding up Sibyl's body, rubbing flesh against flesh. Sensation flooded through me as I came in direct contact with hot, wet flesh. Liam moved his hips, rubbing me up and down against the soaked slit of her pussy.

Every cell of my body twitched and spasmed at the new sensation. It was even better than the tight clasp of Sibyl's mouth.

Fuck her! I screamed the words. I needed more. I needed to know.

"Shut up," Liam snarled at me. He pulled away from Sibyl, and it took all of me not to strangle the idiot. In all of our years together, I'd never shown Liam my full abilities. I hadn't wanted to risk driving him insane. I had no plans to go down with the human.

'What?" Sibyl sounded offended and was hauling her legs up toward her chest. Liam dropped our hands to her knees to stop her.

"Not you, the fucking bane of my existence."

You want to fuck her. I want to fuck her. She wants to be fucked. What is stopping you? I used my limited control of his body to angle myself in Sibyl's direction..

"It's rude to leave me out of the conversation," Sibyl was looking at me. "Especially at a time like this."

Was she seriously telling me I was supposed to talk to her? It went against everything Liam and I had ever encountered. But I liked the idea that she wanted to hear what I had to say, too. It warmed something inside of me.

"I was telling Liam to fuck you already." Her eyes widened and she let out a little laugh. "We all want it. I do not understand the hesitation."

"Good question," Sibyl looked away from me and up at Liam, who just sighed.

"Pardon me for wanting a little foreplay." Liam leaned to the side and got into the drawer on the nightstand. He pulled out a small square packet and ripped it open.

"What is this? No, I do not like this."

Liam continued to roll the suffocating plastic over me until he came to the base, where it began to squeeze me. "Take it off!"

"Absolutely not," Liam said, wrapping his hand around the base of me to smooth the mostly clear film. "I'm not risking an alien baby."

"We don't reproduce like this!" Off! I needed it off.

"Even if that's true, the fact our cum seems to be an aphrodisiac is still a problem." Liam shifts, pulling Sibyl closer.

I begin to argue again, but then I'm there. Back in Sibyl's warmth. I groaned instead. Nothing could be better.

The thought barely formed before Liam pressed forward, squeezing my head into Sibyl's hole.

Fuuuuck.

I embraced the darkness as it squeezed around me. The sensation was unlike anything I'd ever felt before. Better than anything Liam had experienced. It was too much. When Liam moved again and pressed me deeper, I decided if this killed me, I'd die happy.

"No!" My shout was muffled by Sibyl's clasping cunt. But I couldn't keep the objection to myself as Liam slid me out. I never wanted to leave the warm clutch of Sibyl's body.

Before I was pulled free of the wet heat of

Sibyl's body, Liam thrust forward and buried me deep again. The humans were talking to each other, but I couldn't focus on what they were saying.

Sibyl's body clenched again, tighter. It felt like every cell of my being was being compressed. I began to vibrate with sensation.

Chapter 15

Liam

"Oh, fuck," I moaned the words as Sibyl clenched down tight around me. It was so tight, so good.

"Your penis is vibrating." Sibyl said, arching under me and driving me deeper inside of her. "I can't–"

Her words cut off on a moan and her nails dug into my shoulders. My balls drew up tight to my body as I sped toward orgasm.

Get a hold of yourself, man! Bane yelled into my mind. *We are not coming before she does. Grab your balls, think of England, imagine kissing the orange president. I don't give a fuck, get control of it!*

I ground my teeth as I slowed my movements and brought myself back from the edge of orgasm. Sex with Sibyl was unlike anything I'd ever felt before. It was so intense I wasn't sure I could last much longer.

"How do I get you there?" I asked, needing

her to come. Bane was right, we were not coming before her. But if she didn't come soon, I would be embarrassing us. It was just too good.

"Close. Clit." I dove a hand between us until I could circle my thumb on her clit as I continued my jerky, slow thrusts.

"Oh, fuck me." Sibyl clenched around me.

FUCK! Bane shouted in my mind. A thought I couldn't help but second as Sibyl dug her nails into my arms and thrust upward. She began to pulse around me as her orgasm hit. I moaned in relief as I grabbed her hips and began thrusting hard and fast. I was so close to the edge it took almost no time until the pressure in my spine spread out. My balls pulsed as I thrust one last time and held myself deep. My cock exploded.

A sharp sensation spread up my cock. I hissed out a breath at the same time Sibyl let out a yelp. I quickly pulled out of her and stared in horror as purple scales spread their way down my dick.

"What the fuck?" I yanked the condom off and grasped the now bright purple appendage.

"What's happening?" Sibyl said, sitting up and reaching for me. I yanked myself away as a burning sensation took over in my groin. Something was seriously wrong.

"Mating." Bane said, his voice filled with glee.

Chapter 16

Sibyl

Deep purple scales snaked their way up Liam's cock to just below the head, while tentacles of the same color appeared around the base. They wriggled and waved in all directions and reminded me of a sea anemone. I could not decide if I was horrified or curious.

Curiosity won out in the end. I reached out and pressed my fingers into the short tentacles. They immediately closed around my fingers. They were soft and smooth and warm as they brushed over and between my fingers and palm.

"So, that's a thing," I said, moving my hand forward until I could spread my fingers around the base of Liam's penis. I moved them upward, curious about the feel of the scales. The tentacles moved with me. They grew in length to wrap around my wrist as my hand closed over Liam's cock.

The scales were a strange mix of soft and rough. They rippled beneath my grasp as I slid my hand downward toward his body. My pussy clenched as I imagined that strange texture inside of me.

"What the fuck, Bane?" Liam said, thrusting his hips forward. "What is that?"

"My cells are improving your body's design. We are changing to become more compatible for our mate."

"Mate?" The word was a squeak.But seriously, their mate? I was barely handling the fact my crush had a space parasite that made his dick talk and vibrate. I wasn't sure I could handle mating conversations.

I tried to pull my hand free from the tangle of tentacles, but they wrapped tighter around my hand and wrist. I was forced to maintain my hold around Liam's cock.

"There will be no mating!" Liam's voice was firm, but his face was drawn tight. His hips were making tiny thrusts.

"You've chosen to mate. Her body is compatible. Ours is adjusting to bring her maximum pleasure. It's nature."

"There is nothing natural about this!" Liam said, waving his hands at his scaly cock and where my hand was trapped by the tentacles.

Bane let out a long, loud sigh. The sound was so large it caused the penis to shake in my grasp.

"You stupid humans, evolution is natural for every species. Yours just does it over centuries. Aren't we all lucky you have my superior DNA to speed things along?"

"And you think this is what evolution has in mind for my dick?" Liam waved his hands in the direction of his cock. "Will you let SIbyl go already?"

Honestly, I wasn't bothered by our current position. Okay, maybe I would like to move so I wasn't splayed underneath him quite so much, but his cock was fascinating. The texture was almost fish-like, both soft and firm. An upstroke of my hand made the scales shift and rub against my palm.

The tentacles were warm and firm, constantly changing and growing and shrinking depending on my hand position. They weren't slimy, like I'd first expected, but almost felt like additional little penises instead. They alternated between firm and dense, like a hard cock and kind of squishy like a flaccid penis.

Years of reading alien romances had prepared me for this. The endless possibilities were racing through my mind. Some of them must have shown on my face because Liam's mouth dropped open and his eyes went wide as he stared at my face.

"You can't be serious," he said. He looked horrified. I bit the inside of my lower lip and tried not to laugh. "This doesn't bother you?"

"I mean, it's weird as fuck but I guess not."

"There is something wrong with you," Liam gasped as I squeezed him. He grabbed my hand and pulled it off of his cock, fighting the pull of the tentacles. "Knock it the fuck off."

"Says the man with the talking, scaly, be-tentacled penis." I shot back. Liam released me and I shifted out from underneath him and dragged my legs up toward my chest.

"Aw, sweetheart. I didn't mean it like that." Liam reached out and cupped my cheek in his hand. "It's just, this is seriously fucked up."

His eyes were still wild, but he was trying to be gentle with me. I reminded myself I would be panicking if my vagina suddenly grew scales and tentacles. To be honest, I wasn't entirely sure why I wasn't running from the room. I think with anyone else, I would have. But it was Liam. Safe, steady, dependable Liam. My childhood friend. The guy who had given me amazing orgasms.

As weird as it all was, none of it was enough to be a deal breaker for me. To be honest, I couldn't stop wondering what those tentacles could and would do during sex. What the gentle scrape of scales would feel like inside of me.

I even wondered if the heat of his cum would be as potent if it entered me vaginally. The heat of the aphrodisiac had been overwhelming, but it had also been the most pleasure I'd ever experienced. A small, worrisome part of me wanted to feel it again.

"Yeah, it's weird. But you've had a parasitic space mold possessing your penis for over a decade. This is the thing that is going to break you?"

"Do you see my dick?" His voice was high

and strained. "How the hell am I going to explain this thing?"

"Are you planning on showing it to someone else?" I wrapped my arms around my legs. We hadn't talked about it, really. We'd never discussed anything except the chemistry between us. Sure, Liam had been a virgin until an hour ago, but that didn't mean he wanted me specifically.

Liam clearly understood what was going through my brain because the next thing I knew, I was in his lap and wrapped tightly in his arms. The tentacles around his cock were brushing gently against my thighs, ass, and slit.

"Baby, no. I don't mean that. I meant doctors and at the gym. I know we haven't talked about it, but I figured this was more than one night. I hope so, anyway." He brushed a kiss over my forehead. "I don't want anyone but you."

Chapter 17

Liam

I was fucking this up. Sibyl was closing up on me and I couldn't let that happen. Sure, we hadn't talked about it, but I wanted so much more than just one night with her. It was too soon to be thinking long-term, but I'd been fantasizing about her since middle school. There was no way I would be satisfied with just the once.

But seriously, my dick was all kinds of fucked up. While Sibyl didn't seem to be put off by it, I couldn't wrap my head around it. My penis had scales and tentacles, for fuck's sake.

"I have wanted you for so long." Sibyl cupped my face in her hands and pressed a kiss to my lips. "None of this is a deal breaker for me. Don't ask me why, because I should probably be screaming for the government scientists right now, but it doesn't bother me. Yeah, it's weird but it doesn't change what I feel for you."

"You're so strange." I kissed her again. What

started as a brief brush of lips deepened quickly. My body was already hard and ready from Sibyl's hand on me. And now those tentacles were brushing against her bare, wet heat and it was almost too much. They were even more sensitive than my cock. Every brush was like a lightning strike straight up my spine.

"Can you control the tentacles?" Sibyl said against my mouth. She was rocking and shaking in my lap. They were brushing against her soft flesh but avoiding all of the most sensitive places. I tried to direct one toward her clit, but they just kept stroking over her skin.

"I control them," Bane said.

I wasn't sure how I felt about that. I'd gotten used to Bane's presence in my mind and body. Gotten used to his control over my cock and his snarky comments. But I wasn't sure how I felt about him controlling the tentacles currently caressing Sibyl's body.

A pang of jealousy stabbed through me. It was quickly followed by a feeling of ridiculousness. I was jealous of my own fucking penis. I should be happy for anything that brought Sibyl pleasure. And the tentacles were clearly bringing her pleasure.

"Then stop being a fucking tease and please our woman," I growled at him. I started to shift Sibyl off of me, though. I needed to get to the condoms. She stopped me with a hand on my arm.

"I want to try without," her eyes went wide, and she gasped. I moaned as I felt one of the tentacles slide inside of her. Wet, hot, clasping flesh squeezed around it and I went impossibly harder.

"Sibyl," I groaned. I wanted to be inside of her more than anything, but knowing it wasn't smart.

"I have an IUD and I know the risk. You can pull out, if it makes you feel better. But I want to know what it feels like." She shifted, straddled my hips. Her hands came to my shoulders and held there as she waited for me to answer.

Her body was shaking above me as Bane fucked her with the tentacle. It felt good, but my cock was leaking for want of her. I wasn't sure an IUD would be enough against alien DNA-infused cum. I also wasn't sure how she would react to the cum vaginally vs orally, but given the horrible reaction the first time, I wasn't in a rush to find out. I wasn't sure I had the ability to hold myself back from fucking her over and over if she got drugged again.

She slid down and rubbed over me. The tentacle pulled out of her and the head of my cock brushed against her opening. It would be so easy to give in. There were so many reasons not to, but oh, I wanted to.

"Please," Sibyl begged, sliding over the ridge of my dick. She teased me but didn't push me. It was my decision.

"Fuck her already," Bane growled out, throbbing under the press of her pussy. He thumped up against her and she gasped.

Fuck. Oh, fuck. I wasn't going to be able to hold back.

I gripped Sibyl's wide hips and stilled her over me. I angled until my cock rested at her opening. Her eyes flew to mine and held. Her breath caught as I slowly pressed her down over me, onto me.

"Holy shit! Liam!" Her breath whooshed out of her and caught again as she pressed downward to take all of me inside of her. "It feels, oh, my god."

"I know, baby." The clench of her body was indescribable. The flutter of the scales as she pressed downward against them added friction that hadn't been there before. My eyes were nearly rolling back into my head. I wasn't going to last long.

This is pathetic. Bane sneered at me. Sibyl and I both gasped and jumped as one of the tentacles began circling her clenched rear hole. *You've got to work on your stamina.*

I wanted to reply, but I also didn't want to let Sibyl know Bane was questioning my ability to please her. Especially when I was so deep, I was bottoming out with every thrust. Not when she was riding me so hard she was panting and her breasts pressed into my face. Especially not when the tentacle that had been teasing her ass slid home, and she clenched down on me so hard I saw stars. I slid my hand between our bodies so I could circle her clit. If she didn't come soon, Bane's insults would have some merit.

Thankfully, it only took her a second before she threw her head back on a broken scream as she ground down against me. I gripped her hip tight in my hand and thrust up into her. It only took two before her clenching, grasping cunt drove me over the edge into bliss.

Chapter 18

Sibyl

Liam was asleep, but I couldn't settle. My body still hummed with pleasure from the last orgasm. My mind was spinning.

"Go to sleep, baby girl. You need your rest." Bane's voice was sluggish and low. As though he was about to fall asleep as well.

"Do you sleep?" I shifted to my side and laid my head on Liam's chest so I could look down at the soft cock. It was still covered in the soft purple scales. The tentacles were short once again, nestled around the base of the cock. It was unlike anything I'd ever seen, but somehow beautiful.

"Not as you'd call it. But I do rest. You should be." The cock twitched a little but stayed soft against Liam's pelvis and lower belly.

"I'll fall asleep soon." I could feel exhaustion pull at me. While my body still buzzed, my brain was getting sluggish. "Will you, I mean Liam's, or, um, will it stay like that?"

I couldn't stop myself from reaching down and rubbing a hand down the length of him. The scales gently scraped against my hand. I tangled my fingers in the short, stumpy tentacles that reached toward my fingers.

"Evolution rarely goes in reverse." Bane snorted.

"Then you haven't been paying attention to what's happening in this country." I detangled my fingers from the growing tentacles and moved my hand to rest on Liam's chest.

"Humans are primates. Barely evolved creatures. You all are small and weak." Bane twitched against Liam's stomach, but Liam continued his deep, even breathing. It was interesting to see Bane separate from Liam. I was still having trouble wrapping my mind around them being the same, but separate, entities.

"You're space mold. A parasite."

"Here, I am but a parasite." Bane growled, clearly disliking the word. "But in my galaxy, my kind was once feared. Had our star not burned out, we would have conquered planets. We took the smallest form possible to make our escape. Had we landed somewhere more hospitable, we would have remade our home world."

"Why don't you do it here? There are plenty of humans to lure into the mines and inhabit. Why not take over the humans?"

"I like it here." Bane shifted, angling more in my direction. "My kind is intrusive, destructive. They would invade and destroy all of the things

I've come to enjoy about this planet. No, I'll let them stay in the cave and enjoy my time on your planet."

For a moment, I wondered if an alien invasion would be all that bad. America had clearly lost the plot and couldn't be trusted to make rational decisions, based on the felon in chief currently running the country into the ground. Would it be so bad to have an invasive species overthrow the natural order of things? We'd been begging for an alien invasion online for years.

But, while I liked Bane, I doubted I would like a parasitic alien running me around like a puppet on their strings. No, it was better no one ever found out about the colony of aliens in the cave.

"Will your species die out in the cave?" I smothered a yawn with my hand and nestled deeper into Liam's body.

"Eventually. We live for centuries but without the heat of our planet's core, we have no way of reproducing. We are an asexual species, and our reproductive process requires great heat. Eventually, they will die out."

"And you?" My words cut off on another yawn. My body was settling down and lethargy was seeping into my limbs.

"Will die when my host dies."

I nodded. That made sense. A parasite couldn't live without its host. Still, I wondered if it bothered Bane, knowing his lifespan was cut down drastically. Going from centuries to decades couldn't be easy knowledge.

"Don't worry about me, baby girl. Go to sleep," Bane's voice was soft and low. Liam's heart beat steadily under my head. I reached down to wrap my hand around Liam/Bane's soft shaft. It felt strange to be groping Liam in his sleep, but I wanted Bane to have the contact, too.

Vaguely, I wondered if I would ever get used to having two beings sharing Liam's body. If I would always wonder about the logistics. But as I drifted off to sleep, I was hopeful I would have the time and opportunity to try.

Epilogue - Bane

There was nothing better than being stuffed in a warm, wet, willing hole. I shuddered as Sibyl's sweet cunt clenched around me and squeezed so tight I thought I might explode.

I could barely focus on maintaining the pressure and movement she liked on her external sex organs as she moved. Liam was gripping her hips and chanting her name as he laid on his back with Sibyl bouncing on us. I had to hand it to the human. He had gotten better stamina with practice.

I almost never had to yell at him not to come anymore.

Sibyl clenched again, a sure sign she was getting closer to her orgasm. A sensation that never failed to set every one of my cells aflame.

"Oh, fuck." Sibyl yelled, grinding down and throwing her head back. Liam moaned loudly. My own groan was muffled inside the tight clasp of Sibyl's body.

All at once, the three of us came. Cum rushed through me in a brand of hot fluid. It flowed from me in great spurts and painted the inside of Sibyl's body in creamy splashes. I vibrated in pleasure, making the humans moan again.

At last, it stopped and Sibyl slid off of us on shaky legs. She fell to her side on the bed with a laugh that brought a feeling of lightness through our body.

"That was a terrible idea," Sibyl said, stretching out her legs before snuggling close.

"I disagree," I told her. I'd gotten used to speaking aloud when it was just the three of us. Sibyl didn't like it when we had conversations without her and there was an annoying part of me that wanted to please the human as much as Liam did.

"You would," Liam said, but there was none of the usual annoyance in his voice. Orgasms and regular sex had really calmed the guy down. If only he'd listened to me sooner, he could have saved himself years of tension.

Though if he had listened to me sooner, we wouldn't have had Sibyl and there was no way I wanted to miss out on our perfect mate. Especially when her hand slid down to wrap gently around me as we all lay there spent.

"It's bad luck, you know." Sibyl said as she gave me a gentle stroke. "To see the bride before the wedding. I'm pretty sure we just set luck on fire with what we did."

"I'd argue I just got very fucking lucky," Liam said as he tangled a hand in her hair and tugged her in for a kiss. "Though, we probably should have used a condom. I'm going to have fun watching you squirm all day."

Unlike when she ingested it, our cum didn't drive her out of her mind with lust when we came inside of her. But it did leave her high-strung and wanting more for most of the day. She could fuck for hours while riding the high of it, until she collapsed in an exhausted heap.

We'd had a lot of fun figuring out Sibyl's limits with our cum. How much she could ingest without going completely mindless, how many times she could come before passing out. How long she could go without orgasms once she'd taken a load. Sometimes we'd fuck her until Liam couldn't go anymore and then we'd pull out the toys. Other times, we left her aching and wanting until she was begging for me.

No, there was no one more perfect for us than Sibyl. And today, we made her ours in every way.

The emptiness that had left me hollow my entire existence was gone. It was replaced with so much sensation and emotion I had no means of controlling it. I had no desire to.

I was a traitor to my species. If they ever found their way out of the mines, I would be targeted. They would place a bounty on my head and come for me.

Let them come.

The world Liam had shown me, the love Sibyl gave me, made every risk worth it. I would protect them until the end of time. And I would kill anyone who got in my way.

About the Author

Sabrina Cross (she/her) is a neurospicy 80's baby from the middle of nowhere Michigan, where she still lives with her cat. She came into her monster romance era early when she fell in love with Beast from the 1997's X-Men animated series. After discovering sentient object romance in early 2023, Sabrina decided to embrace what she calls her 'Hold My Beer' style of writing and gave into the lifelong dream of being an author. When not writing weird monster/sentient object smut, Sabrina can be found hanging out on social media (@authorsabrinacross), reading, or hoarding office supplies.

Also by Sabrina Cross

Yarn & Monsters Series

A True Love Spell Gone Wrong...

When four friends perform a true love spell, things go terribly wrong. Now they're locked into a deal with the devil and have only a year to find love and happiness or their souls are destined to face the flames. Armed with a demon guardian; Clover, Jasmine, Fern, and Violet are determined to beat the devil and save themselves. Except, this curse might be the best thing that's ever happened to them.

Corny: A F/F Candy Corn Romance

A True Love Spell Gone Wrong...

A Demon Fairy Godmother?

Her very soul on the line. Can Clover still find true love or is she destined to face the flames alone?

Snuggle: A M/F Demon Teddy Bear Romance

A True Love Spell Gone Wrong...

Jasmine is too busy to go to Hell and she's definitely too busy for demon antics. But when her demon "Fairy Godmother" shows up, everything is on the line. Does she have what it takes to get out of the Devil's bargain or is she doomed to face the flames?

Tangled: A M/F Friends-To-Lovers Sentient Object Romance

A True Love Spell Gone Wrong...

Fern is going to Hell. Not metaphorical Hell but actual, physical Hell. But there's one thing she needs to do before she goes. An item she desperately needs to scratch off the bucket list. And she's hoping the demon sent to guard her will be willing to help her out.

Knotted: A M/F Demon Werewolf Romance

A True Love Spell Gone Wrong...

Violet was no witch but that didn't stop her from trying to use magic to find love. When the spell backfired and left her and her friends bound in a deal with the devil, Violet vowed to find a solution. Now, with less than two months until the deal comes due and zero leads, she's facing the fire. The fire comes early in the form of a great black beast in her bed. Does Violet find the love she's been looking for or does Hell claim her soul?

Light Me Up

He was the first man to ever turn me on. When he flipped my switch and lit me up that first time, I knew he was it for me. There would never be another.

Pounded by the Pommel Horse

Elena loves being on top. When the elite gymnast is challenged to defeat her gym rival on the pommel horse, she's up for the task. But is she up for the ride when the pommel horse shapeshifts into a man? A very, very naked Man?

Christmas with the Monster

He's Got a Package for Her... Devynn expected her first holiday without her kids to be difficult. But nothing could have prepared her for what she found under the tree just after midnight.With the help of his magic sack, the furry, green giant promises Devynn all kinds of pleasure. But would one night with the Christmas monster ever be enough?

Sentient Pen 15 from Outer Space

Liam had spent a lot of his childhood obsessed with the legends of the local mines. The abandoned tunnels underground had driven dozens of workers insane and young Liam was desperate to get to the bottom of it. But he found more than he bargained for down there.

Infected by parasitic space mold, Liam has held himself away from relationships for years. When things spark between him and the girl next door, he has no choice but to reveal the truth: his manly appendage is also the bane of his existence.

The Glory Whole Package

Never Piss Off a Witch.

It is a hard-learned lesson and one I may never complete. The endless boredom of my curse is only broken by analyzing the people who use me.

Today I break my silence for the first time and while it might lead to a Happily Ever After, it will never be mine. Not until I've paid for my crimes and earned the forgiveness of the only person I've ever loved.

Getting Railed

"Welcome to Retro Whimsy!"

I hadn't planned on buying anything when entering the new vintage store during my lunch break but somehow found myself leaving with a toy train set.

What could have been written off as an impulse

purchase became so much more when those trains
come to life.

Now I'm stuck dealing with the consequences of a god
curse and deciding if I have what it takes to help
break it.